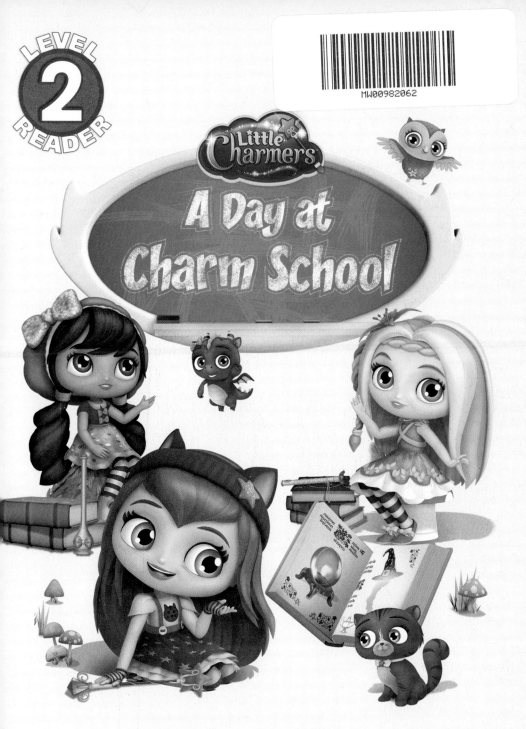

Little Charmers

A Day at Charm School

Adapted by Jenne Simon
from the script by John May & Suzanne Bolch

SCHOLASTIC INC.

Published by Scholastic Inc., *Publishers since 1920*. SCHOLASTIC and associated logos
are trademarks and/or registered trademarks of Scholastic Inc.

The publisher does not have any control over and does not assume any responsibility
for author or third-party websites or their content.

This book is a work of fiction. Names, characters, places, and incidents are either the product of the author's
imagination or are used fictitiously, and any resemblance to actual persons, living or dead, business
establishments, events, or locales is entirely coincidental.

ISBN 978-0-545-93224-0

10 9 8 7 6 5 4 3 2 1   16 17 18 19 20

Printed in the U.S.A.   40
First printing 2016

Book design by Erin McMahon

It was a big day at school for the Little Charmers.

Hazel, Posie, and Lavender were going to learn how to care for plants.

But first, they had recess.

It was time for a fun game, Broom Tag.

Then the Ogre Clock arrived.

"Recess is done!" he called. "Back to classroom fun!"

"Come on," said Posie. "We can't be late for magic bean day!"

Posie loved plants.

Ms. Greensparkle told her class about the project.

"You will grow your magic bean into a magical bean plant," she said.

She asked all the kids to choose a bean.

Posie was more excited than a fairy on the first day of spring!

"Find the bean that is right for you," said Ms. Greensparkle.

Posie watched a bean sparkle and drop into Willow's hand.

Hazel found a bean with lots of energy.

Lavender found one with lots of style.

Posie looked for something special. She found a funny little bean.

"I don't know," said Lavender. "That one looks a little—"

"Itty-bitty," said Posie. "It's perfect!"

8

"Spell the growing spell with me," Ms. Greensparkle told the class.

"Sparkle, sparkle, little bean,
sprout up big and strong.
Grow into the biggest bean we've ever seen,
sprout and grow the whole day long!"

Poof! The beans sprouted into pretty plants. All but Posie's. Hers was tiny!

"Don't worry," she told her friends. "My Sweet Pea is just a late bloomer."

After school, Hazel went back to the classroom.

"Let's give you a little help," she told the bean.

"Twist and shout,
turn you into a giant sprout!
Higglebow, grow, grow,
grow—and grow!"

Poof! The charm worked!
Now Posie's plant was as big as the others.
"That's more like it," said Hazel.
But as Hazel walked away, Posie's plant kept growing . . .

The next day, Posie was in for a *big* surprise.

"Look how big your plant is!" said Ms. Greensparkle. "Somebody has a magic green thumb!"

"Sweet Pea, I knew you'd catch up," said Posie.

"I wish my plant was that big," said Lavender.

"Don't spell your plants bigger," said Ms. Greensparkle. "You don't know what might happen."

Hazel looked at Sweet Pea. Snapdragons! What had she done?!

For the rest of the day, Posie kept Sweet Pea by her side.

During reading, Sweet Pea got smarter—and bigger.

During art, Posie drew a picture of Sweet Pea's long vines.

And during math, Posie counted Sweet Pea's leaves.

"Is it me, or is Posie's plant bigger than before?" Lavender asked Hazel.

Hazel looked worried.

"I did a *Grow, Grow, and Grow* spell for Sweet Pea," she said.

"You Hazeled Sweet Pea?!" said Lavender. "How big will she get?"

"I don't know," said Hazel. "I added an extra 'grow.'"

"That was one 'grow' too many," Lavender sighed.

But Posie did not notice. She was too busy.

Posie gave Sweet Pea water when she was thirsty.

She played her flute when Sweet Pea wanted music.

Who knew plants could sing?

The school day was over, but Posie didn't want to go home.

"I wish I didn't have to leave Sweet Pea at school," she said.

"You could take her home with you," Hazel suggested.

A Sweet Pea playdate! What a charmazing idea!

The next morning, Hazel and Lavender went to Posie's house.

But Posie was still in her pj's!

"What's happening?" asked Lavender.

Posie yawned. "Sweet Pea, that's what."

"Did she grow more?" asked Hazel.

Posie shook her head. "She kept me up all night!

I had to sing to her.

I had to read to her

I had to get her water.

I had to give her lots of hugs!"

"Your Sweet Pea problems will be over soon."
Hazel said. "It's planting day!"

Posie pointed at the vine wrapped around her.
"I don't know if I will even get to school today."

Lavender looked at Hazel. "I told you it was
too many 'grows.'"

"What do you mean?" asked Posie.

"Well, Sweet Pea was so itty-bitty," said Hazel. "I wanted to help her grow a little, so . . ."

Posie stared at her. "You Hazeled my plant?"

"I wanted you to be happy," said Hazel.

Posie sighed. "That was nice, Hazel. But I can't keep this up!"

"Don't worry, Posie," said Lavender. "We'll help."

"There must be a way to fix this," Hazel agreed. "To the Charmhouse!"

The girls charmed Sweet Pea to their clubhouse.

"Are you sure this is just one plant?" asked Lavender.

"Yup! And she's still growing," said Posie. "Watch out!"

Sweet Pea's vines curled around everything in the Charmhouse!

"So much for planting day!" cried Posie. "There's no way we can move her now . . . She's moving me!"

"Maybe we can't move Sweet Pea like this," said Hazel. "But I know how we can!"

Hazel wanted to grow a bunch of little Sweet Peas.

Posie couldn't believe her ears!

"I can't even take care of one Sweet Pea," she moaned.

"It will work. You'll see," said Hazel. "Sparkle up, Charmers!"

"Leaves and stems,
roots and ends,
make our Sweet Pea into
lots of friends!"

Poof! Suddenly, Sweet Pea changed from one big plant into lots of little ones. "Charmazing!" said Posie.

Soon everyone was ready for planting day.
The Little Charmers arrived in style!
"Making Sweet Pea into lots of little plants
was a sparktastic idea!" said Lavender.
"Rain and sun will take care of all the
little Sweet Peas," said Hazel.

"And Posie can get some sleep at night," said Lavender.

Posie smiled at the plants. "I promise I'll come visit all of you!"

Just then, Ms. Greensparkle came over. "Posie's plant is so cute," she said. "But it's still so itty-bitty."

Ms. Greensparkle raised her wand.
"Let's give her a spell, shall we?"

"I wouldn't do that if I were you,"
Hazel said.

"Twist and sprout,
grow, sprout, grow, grow!"

"No!" the Little Charmers shouted.

We ten

But they were too late.

Sweet Pea grew and grew and . . . stole a sip of Ms. Greensparkle's lemonade!

The Little Charmers laughed.

They were happy to have Sweet Pea—and one another.

Because nothing was sweeter than friendship!